This Little Princess
story belongs to
Mila, Edie, Rupert

With my thanks to
San Kiu Lieu and Samantha Riches
who gave me the idea for this story and their
permission to use it when they were at
Keyworth Primary School in London.

This paperback edition first published in 2010 by Andersen Press Ltd.

First published in Great Britain in 1999 by Andersen Press Ltd., 20 Vauxhall Bridge Road, London SW1V 2SA.

Published in Australia by Random House Australia Pty., Level 3, 100 Pacific Highway, North Sydney, NSW 2060.

Copyright © Tony Ross, 1999

The rights of Tony Ross to be identified as the author and illustrator of this work have been
asserted by him in accordance with the Copyright, Designs and Patents Act, 1988.

All rights reserved. Colour separated in Switzerland by Photolitho AG, Zürich.

Printed and bound in China by C&C Offset Printing.

10   9   8   7   6   5   4   3

British Library Cataloguing in Publication Data available.

ISBN 978 1 84270 835 4 (Trade paperback edition)

ISBN 978 1 84939 473 4 (Book People edition)

This book has been printed on acid-free paper

A Little Princess Story

I Want A Sister!

Tony Ross

Andersen Press

"There's going to be someone new in our family,"
said the Queen.

"Oh goody!" said the Little Princess.
"We're going to get a dog."

"No we're not," said the King.
"We're going to have a new baby."

"Oh goody!" said the Little Princess.
"I want a sister!"

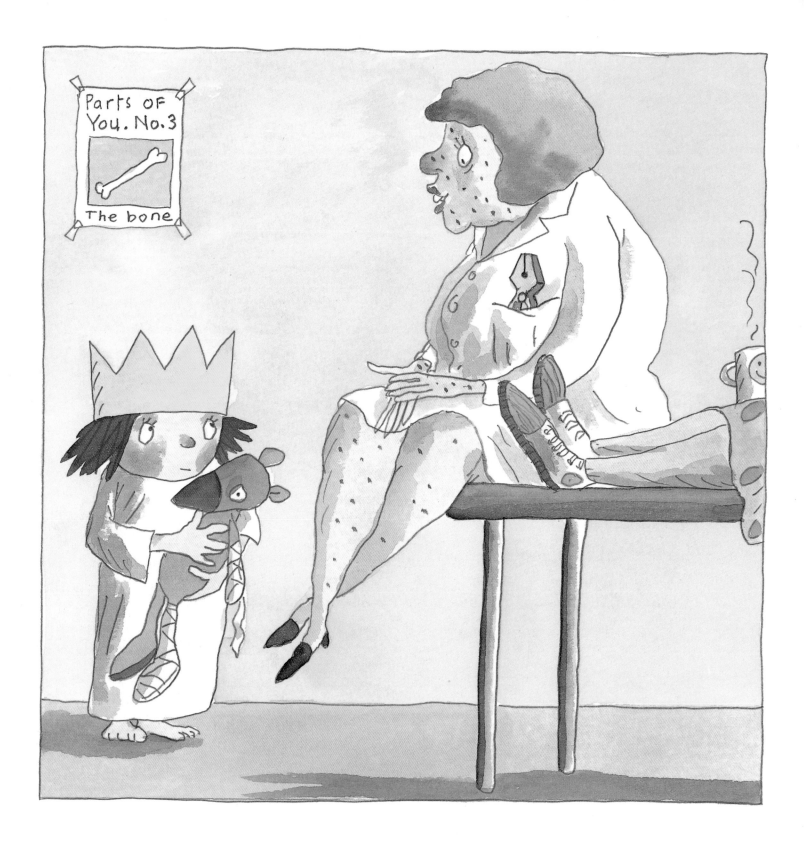

"It may be a brother," said the Doctor.
"You can't choose, you know."

"I don't want a brother," said the Little Princess.
"Brothers are smelly."

"So are sisters," said the Maid.
"Sometimes you smelled AWFUL."

"I don't want a brother," said the Little Princess.
"Brothers are rough."

"So are sisters," said the Admiral.
"Both make TERRIFIC sailors."

"I don't want a brother," said the Little Princess.
"Brothers have all the wrong toys."

"Brothers' toys can be just like yours,"
said the Prime Minister.

"Well," said the Little Princess,
"I JUST DON'T WANT A BROTHER."

"Why?" said everybody.
"BECAUSE I WANT A SISTER," said the Little Princess.

One day, the Queen went to the hospital
to have the new baby.
"Don't forget . . ." shouted the Little Princess,

"... I WANT A SISTER!"

"What if it's a brother?" said her cousin.

"I'll put it in the dustbin," said the Little Princess.

When the Queen came home from hospital,
the King was carrying the new baby.

"Say 'hello' to the new baby," said the Queen.
"Isn't she lovely?" said the Little Princess.

"He isn't a she," said the King. "You have a brother.
A little Prince!"
"I don't want a little Prince," said the Little Princess.
"I want a little Princess."

"But we already have a BEAUTIFUL little Princess,"
said the King and Queen.
"WHO?" said the Little Princess.

"YOU!" said the King and Queen.

"Can my brother have this, now I'm grown up?"
said the Princess.

Other Little Princess Books

I Want My Potty!

I Want My Dinner!

I Want My Light On!

I Want My Present!

I Want to Go Home!

I Want Two Birthdays!

I Want a Party!

I Want to Do it By Myself!

I Want to Win!

I Want My Dummy!

I Don't Want to Go to Hospital!

I Don't Want to Wash My Hands!

LITTLE PRINCESS TV TIE-INS

Can I Keep It?

I Want My New Shoes!

I Don't Want a Cold!

I Want My Tent!

Fun in the Sun!

I Want to Do Magic!

I Want a Trumpet!

I Want My Sledge!

I Don't Like Salad!

I Don't Want to Comb My Hair!

I Want a Shop!

I Want to Go to the Fair!

I Want to Be a Cavegirl!

I Want to Be a Pirate!

I Want to Be Tall!

I Want My Puppets!

I Want My Sledge! Book and DVD